The POOH SONG BOOK

BOOKS FOR BOYS AND GIRLS
BY A. A. MILNE
with Decorations by E. H. SHEPARD:

WHEN WE WERE VERY YOUNG

NOW WE ARE SIX

WINNIE-THE-POOH

THE HOUSE AT POOH CORNER

THE CHRISTOPHER ROBIN STORY BOOK

THE POOH SONG-BOOK

E. P. DUTTON & CO., INC.

The
POOH SONG BOOK

containing

THE HUMS OF POOH
THE KING'S BREAKFAST
and
FOURTEEN SONGS
from
WHEN WE WERE VERY YOUNG

Words by
A. A. MILNE
Music by
H. FRASER-SIMSON
Decorations by
E. H. SHEPARD

New York
E. P. DUTTON AND COMPANY, INC.

The Pooh Song Book first published 1961 by E. P. Dutton & Co., Inc.

The Hums of Pooh copyright 1930 by E. P. Dutton & Co., Inc.,
Renewal copyright 1958 by Mrs. Daphne Milne.

The King's Breakfast and Fourteen Songs copyright 1924, 1925
by E. P. Dutton & Co., Inc., Renewal copyright 1952 by A. A. Milne.

All rights reserved. Printed in the U.S.A.

&

No part of this book may be reproduced in any form without permission in writing from the publisher, except by a reviewer who wishes to quote brief passages in connection with a review written for inclusion in a magazine, newspaper or broadcast.

j784.8 Fras

Fraser-Simson, Harold,
1878-1944.
The Pooh song book.

[1961]

San Francisco Public Library

Main Children's Room

Library of Congress Catalog Card Number: M61-1020

CONTENTS

&

&

THE HUMS OF POOH

Dedicated by
H. F-S and A. A. M.
to
Cicely Fraser-Simson

—

As Pooh is inspired by a hum or a whistle he
Hears in the tops of the Trees,
As Eeyore is moved by the crunch of the thistle he
Pulls at his negligent ease,
So we were inspired by the humour which Cicely
Brought to the singing of these.

Introduction

If you have read (and I don't know why you should, but it will make it very awkward for me if you haven't) two books called *Winnie-the-Pooh* and *The House at Pooh Corner,* then you will need no introduction to this one. For when you see it, you will say (at least, I hope you will) "Ah, here it is at last!" And here it is.

But if you haven't read these other two books, then, as I say, you have made it very awkward for me. Because what I want to say, and keep on saying, is "What! You *haven't?* Well! What *have* you been doing all this time?" — and I oughtn't to say this, because (you may as well know; it's bound to come out) I am the author of those two books. I was taught in the nursery (perhaps wrongly) that "Self-praise is no recommendation" — (one "c" and two "m's." Some people do it the other way) — but sometimes I think that if one doesn't praise oneself, and there's nobody else noticing, who *is* going to do it? When I write an Introduction for somebody else's book, I never let go the pen until all my readers are trooping off to the bookshops, and saying "I want two copies of all the books which this man, I've forgotten his name, has written," but the bother is that I can never get anybody else to write an Introduction to *my* books. They say "Oh, no, you can do it so much better yourself"; and I daresay I can; but I can't Let Myself Go as they could. I did say to Mr. Fraser-Simson, "Suppose we have two Introductions, and *I'll* tell everybody how good the music is, and *you* tell everybody how good the words are, and then nobody can possibly say we are being conceited," but he wouldn't. He says he can't write. I suppose he puts two "c's" and one "m" — a pity.

Very well, then, I've got to do it myself, and this is what I've got to explain. In those two books which you haven't read . . . . . WHICH YOU HAVEN'T READ . . . . . no, no, let us hush it up — which you haven't read — there was a Bear called Pooh, who lived in the Forest, and hummed as he went about his way. If you had read the books (I am sorry, but I must say it again) you would know all about these hums of his, and just what part of each book each one came in, and what Pooh was doing at the time, and who Tigger and Eeyore and Christopher Robin were. And as you looked through this book, recognizing old friends, you would say of each one, "I've often wondered what the tune of *this* was, and now I know." But, as it is, you will be saying, "Rumty Tiddle-y tiddle-y tum, rum tiddle-y tum tum — oh, no it's B *flat* — tum *tum*. A very pretty tune, but what's it all *about*?" So at the beginning of each song I have explained, as quickly as possible, what it *is* all about.

And, turning back to those sensible people, those dear friends, those adventurers, who *have* read the books and know them by heart, perhaps it would be as well if you too, when you sing these songs in public, were first to read aloud these little explanations. For you never know. People are funny; and the old gentleman with whiskers in the middle of the third row *may* take the Pooh books to bed with him every night . . . or he *may* have thought that this was a meeting of the Royal Asiatic Society. So, if the policeman misdirected him at the corner, or he thought it was Tuesday, you can spare him something of the surprise by not sailing into the song until you have given him these few words of warning.

And, finally, to those same dear friends, (since this may be the last time that the word "Pooh" will leave my nib) may I say, "Thank you for having loved him." He will be very proud if you sing his songs, and so keep him for ever in your memory.

A. A. MILNE

CONTENTS

THE HUMS OF POOH

Isn't it Funny . . . .

One day when Pooh was out walking, he came to a very tall tree, and from the top of the tree there came a loud buzzing noise. Well, Pooh knew what that meant — honey; so he began to climb the tree. And as he climbed, he sang a little song to himself. Really it was two little songs, because he climbed twenty-seven feet nine-and-a-half inches in between the two verses. So if the second verse is higher than the first, you will know why.

Isn't it Funny . . . .
Buzzily
mf
Is - n't it fun - ny How a bear likes hon - ey?
Buzz! Buzz! Buzz! I won - der why he does?
sf
tr

It's a ve-ry fun-ny thought that, if Bears were Bees, They'd
sf
mp
build their nests at the bot-tom of trees. And that be-ing so (if the
Bees were Bears) We should-n't have to climb_ up_ all these
stairs.
f

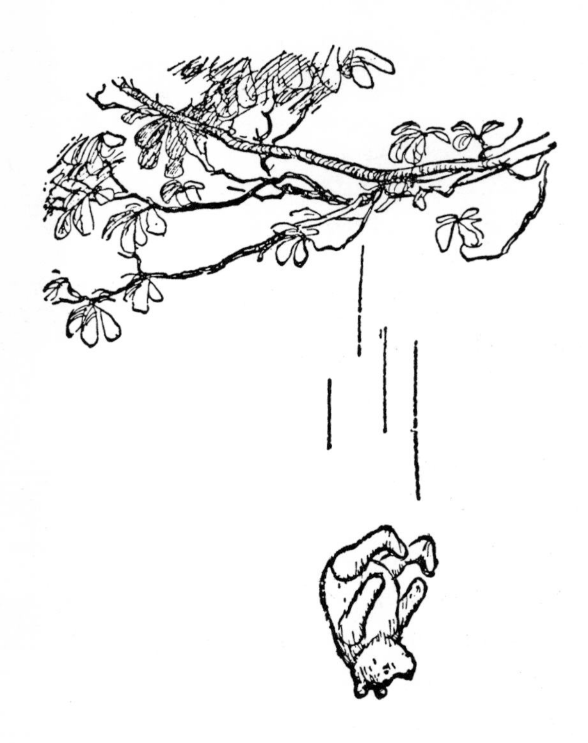

How Sweet to be a Cloud . . . .

When Pooh had fallen from the top of the honey-tree to the bottom (in the quickest time that anybody had ever done it in) he picked himself out of the gorse-bush, and tried to think of another way of getting to the honey. So he thought of floating up to the top of the tree on the end of a blue balloon, and trying to look like a Small Cloud in a very blue sky. And so as to deceive the bees entirely, he sang a small Cloud Song, such as a cloud might sing. Here it is . . . .

How Sweet to be a Cloud . . . .
Floatingly
p
How
sweet to be a Cloud Float-ing in the Blue! Ev'-ry lit-tle cloud
Al-ways sings a-loud. "How sweet to be a Cloud
mf

Float - ing in the Blue!"
"How sweet to be a Cloud
Float - ing in the Blue!"
It makes him ve - ry proud
To
rit.
a tempo
be a lit - tle Cloud.
How sweet to be a Cloud
Float - ing in the
mf
rit.
p a tempo
Blue!

It's very, very Funny . . . .

One day Pooh and Piglet were trying to catch a Heffalump, and they decided that the best way was to dig a Heffalump Trap and put something in it which Heffalumps liked. And Piglet thought that what they liked best was Honey, because then Pooh would have to go back to his house and get some ; and Pooh thought that they liked Haycorns best, because then Piglet would have to go back ; but Piglet thought first. So Pooh went back and got his last pot of honey for the Trap. And in the night he woke up feeling very hungry, and went to his empty cupboard . . . and when he couldn't find any he sang this song.

It's very, very Funny....

Cottleston Pie

This is a song which you sing when anybody says anything which you don't quite understand. You could say "What?" or "I beg your pardon," but Pooh always used to sing *Cottleston Pie*, which is a song he made up for singing when his brain felt fluffy.

Cottleston Pie
Wonderingly
f
mp
Cot - tle - ston,
Cot - tle - ston, Cot - tle - ston Pie. A fly can't bird, but a
bird can fly. Ask me a rid - dle and I re - ply:
mf

"Cot - tle - ston, Cot - tle - ston, Cot - tle - ston Pie."
Cot - tle - ston,
Cot - tle - ston, Cot - tle - ston Pie. A fish can't whis - tle and
neith - er can I. Ask me a rid - dle and I re - ply:
"Cot - tle - ston, Cot - tle - ston, Cot - tle - ston Pie."
mf
f

Cot - tle - ston, Cot - tle - ston, Cot - tle - ston Pie. Why does a
mp
chick - en, I don't know why. Ask me a rid - dle and
mf
I re - ply: "Cot - tle - ston, Cot - tle - ston, Cot - tle - ston
Pie!"
f
p
f

Lines Written by a Bear of Very Little Brain

The title of this song is *Lines Written by a Bear of Very Little Brain*, and as that describes it, I won't say any more about it, except that Kanga said "Yes it is, isn't it?" just as the fifth verse was beginning. So we shall never know what happened on Friday.

Lines Written by a Bear of Very Little Brain

-bod - y knows If those are these or these are those.
f
On Wednes-day, when the
mf
mp
sky is blue, And I have noth - ing else to do, I some-times won - der
cresc.
if it's true That who is what and what is who.
mf
sf
On Thurs-day, when it starts to freeze And
mp

hoar - frost twink - les on the trees, How ve - ry rea - di - ly one sees That
cresc.
these are whose- but whose are these?
On Fri - day-
On Fri - day-
(Spoken)
On Fri - day-
"What did happen on Friday?"

Sing Ho! for the Life of a Bear . . . .

This is a song sung by Pooh when he feels Ho-ish. Some people, when they feel like this, either look about for somebody to push over, or else they break something accidentally, but Pooh works it off by singing a small Ho-song.

Sing Ho!
for the Life of a Bear. . . .

got a lot of hon - ey on my nice clean paws! Sing Ho! for a Bear! Sing
mf
Ho! for a Pooh! And I'll have a lit - tle some - thing in an
hour or two! Sing Ho! for a Bear! Sing Ho! for a Pooh! And I'll
f
have a lit - tle some - thing in an hour or two!

They all went off to discover the Pole . . . .

This is the song which Pooh sang on the Expotition to the North Pole, led by Christopher Robin. When he got to the end of the first verse Christopher Robin said " Hush ! " (because they were coming to a dangerous place) which explains why there isn't a second verse.

They all went off to discover the Pole . . . .

all went too— And where the Pole— was none of them knew... Sing
Hey! for Owl and Rab-bit and all! Sing
Hey! for Owl and Rab-bit and all his friends and re-la-tions and Pig-let and Pooh and
Kan-ga and Roo And Ee-yore and Chris-to-pher Rob-in and all!
dim.
p
poco a poco cresc.
f
sf

NorTH PoLE
DICSovERED By
POOH
POOH FoUND IT

3 Cheers for Pooh . . . .

This is an Anxious Pooh Song. Pooh Bear was anxious, because Christopher Robin was giving a party to celebrate something which Pooh had done, and Pooh was afraid that perhaps none of the others at the party would know about his Brave Rescue of Piglet (which is what he had done), and say "Why?" when Christopher Robin said "Three Cheers for Pooh!" or whatever you say after a Brave Rescue. So he made up a song about how awkward it would be if everybody said "Why?" and "Who?" and "I didn't hear." This is the song.

3 Cheers for Pooh . . . .

talk-ing of Pooh— (Of who?) Of Pooh! (I'm sor-ry I keep for-get - ting.)
p
Well, Pooh was a Bear of E-
mp
-nor-mous Brain—(Just say it a-gain!) Of e-nor-mous brain—(Of e-nor-mous what?) Well, he ate a lot, And I
don't know if he could swim or not, But he man-aged to float on a sort of boat (On a sort of what?) Well, a
cresc.
sort of pot— So now let's give him three hear-ty cheers (So now let's give him three hear-ty which-es!) And
f
poco rit.
mf

hope he'll be with us for years and years, And grow in health and wis-dom and rich-es!
a tempo
poco rit.
a tempo
f
mp
f
cheers for Pooh! (For who?) For Pooh- 3 cheers for Bear! (For where?) For Bear- 3 cheers for the won-der-ful
p
f
p
f
mp
cresc.
Win-nie the Pooh! (Just tell me, some-bod-y- WHAT DID HE DO?)
f
mp

The more it Snows . . . .

This is Pooh's favourite song, and mine too. It is described in the catalogues as an "Outdoor Hum for Snowy Weather" and there is a special footnote by Mr. Brown, the manager, to say that the chorus can be sung separately while doing stoutness exercises, but really anybody can sing it anywhere. It is very good for keeping the feet warm, which is really why Pooh made it up.

The more it Snows . . . .
March time
f
mf
The
more it SNOWS - tid - de - ly - pom, The more it GOES - tid - de - ly -
- pom The more it GOES - - tid-de-ly-pom On Snow - ing On
47

Snow - ing. And no - bod - y KNOWS - tid - de - ly - pom, How
cold my TOES - tid - de - ly - pom How cold my TOES - - tid - de - ly - pom Are
Grow - ing, Are Grow - ing. Tra - la - la,
tra - la - la, Tra - la - la, tra - la - la, Rum - tum - tid - dle - um - tum.
Tid - dle - id - dle, tid - dle - id - dle, Tid - dle - id - dle, tid - dle - id - dle,
p

Rum - tum - tum - tid-dle - um.
Tra - la - la,
tra - la - la,
Tra-la-la,
tra-la-la,
Rum - tum - tid-dle-um-tum.
Tid - dle - id - dle,
tid - dle - id - dle,
Tid - dle - id - dle,
tid - dle - id - dle,
Rum - tum - tum - tid-dle - um.
f
fz

What shall we do about poor little Tigger? . . . .

Tigger was a very Bouncy Animal, and when he first came to the Forest, it was a long time before anybody could discover what he liked for breakfast. Pooh made up a song about it. He put in the last two lines because Piglet, who was a Very Small Animal, thought that Tigger bounced too much.

What shall we do about poor little Tigger? . . . .

And
all the good things which an an - i - mal likes Have the
p
wrong sort of swal-low or too ma - ny spikes. But what -
-ev - er his weight in pounds, shil - lings and ounc - es, He al - ways seems big - ger be -

-cause of his bounces.
bounces.

I could spend a happy morning . . .

One day Pooh sat in the Sun, and wondered what to do. First of all he thought he would go and see Kanga and Roo . . . . and then he thought he would go and see Rabbit (who always said " Help Yourself" and " What about another slice ? ") . . . . and then he thought that most of all, he would like to see his favourite friend, Piglet. In the three verses of this song you can hear him trying to make up his mind. If the last verse isn't very good, you must remember that it was the sort of lazy, sunny day when nobody really bothers.

I could spend
a happy morning . . .
Consideringly
mf
mp
I could spend a hap - py morn - ing See - ing Roo, I could
spend a hap - py morn - ing Be - ing Pooh. For it does - n't seem to mat - ter, If I
don't get an - y fat - ter (And I don't get an y fat - ter), What I do.
mf

Oh, I like his way of talk-ing, yes, I
do. It's the nic-est way of talk-ing Just for two. And a
poco cresc.
Help-your-self with Rab-bit Tho' it may be-come a hab-it, Is a
pleas-ant sort of hab-it For a Pooh.
I could spend a hap-py morn-ing See-ing Pig-let. And I

could - n't spend a hap - py morn - ing Not see - ing Pig - let. And it
does - n't seem to mat - ter If I don't see Owl and Ee - yore (or any of the others), And I'm
colla voce.
not going to see Owl or Eeyore (or any of the others) Or Chris - to - pher
Rob - in.
a tempo
f

Oh, the Butterflies are flying . . . .

This song is known as "Noise, by Pooh." He "Sort of made it up" one spring day. As he explained to Rabbit, "It isn't Brain, because You Know Why, Rabbit ; but it comes to me sometimes," and Rabbit who never let things come to him, but always went and fetched them, said "Ah!" encouragingly.

Oh, the Butterflies
are flying....
Happily
p
Oh, the but-ter-flies are fly-ing, Now the win-ter days are dy-ing, And the
prim-ros-es are try-ing To be seen. And the tur-tle-doves are coo-ing, And the
woods are up and do-ing, For the vi-o-lets are blue-ing, In the

green.
Oh, the hon-ey-bees are gumming On their
lit-tle wings, and humming That the summer, which is com-ing, Will be fun.
And the
cows are al-most coo-ing, And the tur-tle-doves are moo-ing, Which is
why a Pooh is pooh-ing In the sun.
For the
spring is real-ly spring-ing; You can see the sky-lark sing-ing, And the
p

blue-bells which are ring-ing, Can be heard. And the cuc-koo is-n't coo-ing, But he's
cuck-ing and he's oo-ing, And a Pooh is sim-ply pooh-ing Like a
bird.
rit.
a tempo
rall. al fine.

If Rabbit was bigger . . . .

One day Rabbit decided that It Couldn't Go On Any Longer. Tigger was getting too Bouncy and must be unbounced. And when he heard this, Pooh made up a very quiet Hum which he hummed to himself.

If Rabbit was bigger . . . .

Humming
If Tig-ger was smal-ler, Then
a tempo
Tig-ger's bad hab-it Of bounc-ing at Rab-bit Would mat-ter No long-er,
Humming
If Rab-bit Was tal-ler.
rit.
a tempo
(Spoken)
If Rab-bit Was tal-ler.
But he isn't!
rit.
a tempo
p

This Warm and Sunny Spot . . . .

This song was made up by Pooh in a Thoughtful Spot where he and Piglet used to meet, but if I say any more about it, the Explanation will be longer than the Song.

This Warm and Sunny Spot....

Oh, both-er, I for - got, Oh,
both-er, I for - got,
mf
It's Pig - let's too. Oh, both - er, I for -
p
(Spoken)
-got It's Pig let's too. "Sorry, Piglet!"
rit.

I lay on my Chest . . . .

Pooh and Piglet were having tea with Owl one blusterous day, and suddenly Owl's house was blown down, and all the furniture in the sitting-room rushed up to the ceiling and the ceiling rushed down to the floor, and nobody knew where anybody else was. For a long time Pooh was completely missing, and it wasn't until one of the chairs began to talk that Piglet thought of looking in the right place. This is the song which Pooh made up while he was waiting to be rescued.

I lay on my Chest . . . .

noth - ing par - tic - u - lar seemed to come. My
cresc.
f
mp
face was flat On the floor, and that Is all ve - ry well for an
ac - ro - bat; But it does - n't seem fair To a Friend - ly Bear To
rit.
stif - fen him out with a bask - et - chair. And a
rit.
f

sort of sqoze Which grows and grows Is not too nice for his
mp
poor old nose, And a sort of squch Is much too much For his
cresc.
neck and his mouth and his ears_ and such.
rit.
mf
piu mosso
f

Here lies a Tree . . . .

This is a Respectful Pooh Song in praise of Piglet, and describes so exactly what happened when Owl's house blew down that I shan't say any more about it.

Here lies a Tree . . . .
Dramatically
f
Here lies a tree which Owl (a
p
bird) Was fond of when it stood on end, And Owl was talk-ing to a friend Called Me (in case you had-n't
heard) When something Oo oc-curred. For lo! the wind was blust-er - ous And flat-tened out his fav-'rite
more brightly
mp
tree; And things looked bad for him and we— Looked bad, I mean, for he and us— I've nev-er known them
poco cresc.

wuss. Then Pig-let (PIG-LET) thought a thing: "Courage!" he said. There's al-ways
f
p
hope. I want a thin-nish piece of rope. Or, if there is-n't an-y, bring A thick-ish piece of
with more spirit
string." So to the let-ter-box he rose, While Pooh and Owl said "Oh!" and "Hum!" And where the let-ters al-ways
poco cresc.
come (Called "LETTERS ON-LY") Pig-let sqoze His head and then his toes.
f
O gal-lant Pig-let (PIG-LET)! Ho! Did Pig-let trem-ble? Did he blinch? No, no, he strug-gled inch by
p
3

excitedly
inch Through LETTERS ON-LY, as I know Be-cause I saw him go. He ran and ran, and then he
stood And shout-ed, "Help for Owl, a bird, And Pooh, a bear!" un-til he heard The oth-ers com-ing through the
poco cresc.
As when singing Grand Opera
wood As quick-ly as they could. "Help-help and Res-cue!" Pig-let cried, And
f
mf
showed the oth-ers where to go. Sing ho! for Pig-let (PIG-LET) ho! And soon the door was o-pened wide,
cresc.
f
mp
p
And we were both out-side! Sing ho! for Pig-let, ho! Ho!
f
sf
sf

Christopher Robin is going . . . .

This song oughtn't to be in the book really, because it was written by Eeyore, the old grey donkey. "Hitherto," as he explained to the other animals, "all the Poetry in the Forest has been written by Pooh, a bear with a Pleasing Manner but a Positively Startling Lack of Brain," and when he had read it to them, and Pooh had said admiringly, "It's much better than mine," Eeyore explained modestly that it was meant to be. But I don't think it is ; and I put it in here, in a book of Pooh Songs partly because it shows that Poetry and Hums are more difficult than people suppose, and partly because it says good-bye to Pooh's great friend, Christopher Robin.

Christopher Robin is going....
Wistfully
con Ped.
Chris-to-pher Rob-in is go-ing. At least I think he is. Where? No-bod-y knows. But he is go-ing— I mean he goes (To rhyme with "knows") Do we care? (To rhyme with "where") We
EOR

do ve - ry much.
I haven't got a rhyme for that "is" in the second line yet.
Pooh
Both-er.) (Now I haven't got a rhyme for that bother. Bother.)
Those two bothers will have to rhyme with each other.
mf
Buth-er. The fact is this is more difficult than I thought I ought— (Very good indeed) I
p
ought To be-gin a-gain, But it's eas - i - er to stop.
3
Chris-to - pher Rob - in, good - bye, I (Good) I And all your

friends sends I mean all your friend send– (Very awkward this, it keeps going wrong) Well,
an-y-how, we send Our love– we send Our love– we send Our love– Well,
an-y-how, we send, our love END.
poco rit.
pp

THE KING'S BREAKFAST

INTRODUCTION

In which various matters are explained, and the Old English song, "Feed-My-Cow," is now given for the first time.

BEFORE we start singing *The King's Breakfast*—and I have had a lozenger in my mouth all the morning, in the hope of being in good voice—there is a little matter which has to be settled between us. You will remember that when the King asked the Queen for butter, the Queen naturally asked the Dairymaid, and that the Dairymaid, having no butter with her, promised to ask the Cow. So far, so good. But the Dairymaid, in promising, used a very curious expression, She said:

"I'll go and tell the Cow now,
Before she goes to bed."

You will not be surprised to hear that, as the result of these words, the whole world has been asking, *Why did the Cow go to bed at breakfast time?*

Now in this matter there have been, for many years, two schools of thought. The Grumphiter School (called after Dr. James Grumphiter, of Ladbroke Grove) holds that, for reasons as yet unascertained, the Alderney cow was in the habit of having a short nap in the forenoons, probably between the hours of ten and twelve. At noon she was awakened; and, after a drink of water and a couple of health biscuits, was led back into the fields again; from which point in the day she followed the routine of the ordinary cow. In other words, Dr. Grumphiter thinks that Alderney was a special kind of cow who required special care in the mornings.

An entirely different view of the matter is taken by the Cadwallader School. ("Cadwallader," I should explain, is pronounced "Calder," and was so spelt until 1903, when the Professor married again: "School" of course, is pronounced "Scool," the "h" being kept quiet). The Cadwallader School, led by Professor H. J. Cadwallader, of Dunstable University, is of opinion that "the transactions narrated in the poem cover a period of, approximately, twenty-four hours, and that actually *two* breakfasts have come within the purview of the historian." It is a pity he uses such long words, but no doubt you see what he means.

Let us consider this Cadwallader Theory for a moment. A time-table of events would seem to go something like this:

Monday, 9 a.m. King and Queen at breakfast. King realizes that there is only enough butter for that day's meal, assuming (as usual) that the Queen is not hungry. He helps himself to the last of the pat, saying to her Majesty, "Don't forget the butter for the (to-morrow's) royal slice of bread." The Queen says, "I won't," but she is thinking of something else.

" 10 *a.m.*—6 *p.m.* The Queen attends to her customary royal duties, Monday being a particularly busy day, what with Receptions, Executions, the Washing, and so forth.

Monday,	*6 p.m.*	The Dairymaid asks for orders. The Queen, interrupted in her toilet, says that butter will be wanted for to-morrow's breakfast. The Dairymaid promises to tell the Cow now, before the latter goes to bed.
Monday,	6.15 *p.m.*	Cow suggests marmalade instead.
"	6.30 *p.m.*	Dairymaid assures Queen that marmalade is tasty.
"	6.31 *p.m.*	Queen says "Oh," and decides to wear the purple after all.
"	10 *p.m.*	Their Majesties retire to rest.
. .	. .	. . . . . .
Tuesday,	8 *a.m.*	Their Majesties rise.
"	9 *a.m.*	Their Majesties descend the royal staircase into the Banqueting Hall. Fanfare of trumpets. As the last note dies away, Queen says to King, "Talking of the butter for the royal slice of bread, many people think that marmalade is nicer, would you like to try a little marmalade instead?"
"	9.5 *a.m.*	King says "Bother."
"	9.6 *a.m.*	King says "Oh, deary me."
"	9.7 *a.m.*	King sobs, and goes back to bed.

After which, it is pretty plain sailing. The Queen comforts His Majesty, and hurries to the Dairymaid; in a trice the Dairymaid is with the Alderney; in a jiffy the Alderney, repentant after a good night's rest, gives the Dairymaid the necessary butter; and in a brace of shakes the Dairymaid has brought the butter to the Queen. Whereupon:

"The Queen took
The Butter
And brought it to
His Majesty . . ."
—and so, calmly, to the long-wished-for end.

Well, that is the Cadwallader Theory. But why, if these be the facts of the matter, has the poet (to use the local name for this sort of man) not put them more clearly before us? Why did he not tell us the truth? Thus:

The King asked
The Queen, and
The Queen wasn't
Listening:
"Can I have some butter for
To-morrow's slice of bread?"
The Queen said
"I won't dear . . .
Stockings and
A night-cap—
Or wear the cap another week
And send the shawl
Instead?"
The Queen took
The washing . . .

But we need not go any further with it. The Professor suggests that the poet wrote as he did, because he had a long story to tell, *but very little paper to tell it on.* It was necessary for him, therefore, to squeeze the events of twenty-four hours into a space of five minutes, regardless of historical accuracy. And the Professor adds in a thoughtful footnote: *"Poets are like this."*

We have to decide, then, which of these two schools of thought has found the right explanation of the Dairymaid's words. And the answer is, "Neither." The truth of the matter is simply this: The Alderney had chased the king across two turnip fields the day before, and, *as a punishment,* had been sent to bed immediately after breakfast. She hadn't meant any harm, as you will know if you have ever read an old song which was sung in those days, and which is supposed to have referred to this adventure of the King's. Here it is—you will find the music for it on another page.

Feed—My—Cow

I

I went down to feed—my—cow,
(Feed—my—cow,
Feed—my—cow)
I went down to feed my cow
At ten o'clock in the morning.

II

She looked out and shook—her—head
(Shook—her—head,
Shook—her—head)
She looked out and shook her head
At ten o'clock in the morning.

III

I said bravely, "Here—I—come!"
(Here—I—come,
Here—I—come)
I said bravely "Here I come,
At ten o'clock in the morning."

IV

She looked out and shook-her-horns,
(Shook—her—horns,
Shook—her—horns)
She looked out and shook her horns
At ten o'clock in the morning.

V

I said bravely, "Not—so—close!"
(Not—so—close,
Not—so—close)
I said bravely "Not so close
At ten o'clock in the morning."

VI

She came out and shook-her-tail,
(Shook—her—tail,
Shook—her—tail)
She came out and shook her tail,
At ten o'clock in the morning.

VII

I went back to ask—the—time
(Ask—the—time
Ask—the—time)
I went back to ask the time
At ten o'clock in the morning.

VIII

She came too, to—ask—the—time
(Ask—the—time
Ask—the—time)
She came too, to ask the time
At ten o'clock in the morning.

IX

We both ran, but *I—asked—first,*
(I—asked—first,
I—asked—first),
We both ran, but I asked first:
'Twas ten o'clock in the morning.

Well, that was how it happened, and in the afternoon, when the King felt rested, he decided to give the cow a very severe punishment. So it was ordered (and the King wrote it out and sealed it and signed it with his own hand) that on the very next day the Alderney should go to bed "at ten o'clock in the morning."

Now then, having got that off our minds, we can clear our throats. But before we begin to sing it, I think I ought to tell you how to *say* a poem like this. It doesn't matter whether you are reciting it, reading it, acting it, or even singing it, there is one way only of doing it, and that is—*on tiptoe.* This story of *The King's Breakfast* is not a walk or a slide or a slither, it is a ballet-dance. I have heard people recite it; and I have heard them say, with a great deal of expression, as though they were reading *The Decline and Fall of the Roman Empire* aloud to a sick friend:

"The King asked the Queen (*swallow*) and the Queen asked the Dairymaid . . ."

Now that is not how it was written. It is always a good idea to suppose that, when somebody writes something in a certain way, this is the way in which he wants it said.

The King asked—
The Queen and—
The Queen asked—
The Dairymaid—

It is a ballet-dance, in which each step is distinct, not a waltz, where one step slides into the next; formal, like a Dutch garden, not a riot in a herbaceous border. And, above all, it is "expressionless" as far as meaning goes. All that the speaker has to express is the rhythm and the shape of it; the words have very simple definite meanings of their own, and can take care of themselves quite nicely. Don't be afraid of saying "and" at the end of the second line; the second and third words have the same value, and you need not be alarmed because one is a Royal noun, and the other is a common conjunction. I know that you are in the habit of saying " 'nd"—"Jack 'nd Jill," and quite right too. But there will be no sort of panic among the guests if, on this occasion only, you say "and," nor will anybody wonder what the word means. Only mind that you do say "and," and not "nand." "The Queen nand"—if you say this, you're slithering again, not tip-toeing. What I want you to do is to give each word which you stress a "ting," and then leave it; touch, and away—as if it were a hot poker.

And again, remember: no "expression." No, not even when "he kissed her tenderly," and "slid down the banisters." If these words are "funny," they will be twice as funny for being said in just the same voice, as if one way was as good as and natural as another for celebrating the appearance of the butter. Indeed, the more I think of it, the more I am convinced that a Russian who knew the meaning of no word of English, but only how to pronounce it, would be the ideal person to recite *The King's Breakfast*. So if you like, pretend that you are a Russian.

At the moment, however, you are not to recite, but to sing. Now when the composer wrote the music, I wanted it to be printed in the same shape as the words, so that when it was published it would look like a washing-book, long and narrow. Apparently, you can't do that; it falls off the piano just as you get to the high note. So here it is, printed in the ordinary way. But I beg you, accompanist and singer, to play and sing it as I have tried to explain, in short lines. No doubt there are musical reasons why you won't be able to do this altogether, but keep the idea in your heads, as you go along.

And now our guests are closing their eyes one

by one, and it is time we woke them up. We begin with a short musical introduction, and end with a dance. I have explained above the music what the introduction is about, though, for many people, no doubt, it explains itself. If you like to read this out as you play, do so—and good luck to you.

A. A. Milne.

THE KING'S BREAKFAST

*When sung without action the bars between this point and the * on page 3 may be omitted.

Hooray, He's found it!!
He comes down the
"Bother !"
a tempo
stairs two at a time.
"Dear! dear! the Queen's late
again! Sound the gong!"
The Queen says
"Coming!"
She trips down the stairs gracefully.
But His Majesty is still a little annoyed about it.
"Very sorry"
"Granted"
"Very sorry"
"Very sorry"
cresc.
"Granted"
accel.
"GRANTED !"
"Very sorry"
"GRANTED!!!"

They pull themselves together ——— and make a State Entry
a tempo
sfp
f
to music provided by ———
The Court Musician — a hungry sort of man.
dim.
p
The
The Queen sits down.
The King follows.
"What! no butter?"
mf
sf
mf

King asked The Queen, and The Queen_ asked The Dai - ry-maid:
"Could we have some but-ter for the Roy - al slice of bread?" The
Queen asked The Dai - ry-maid; The Dai - ry-maid Said, "Cer-tain-ly, I'll
go and tell The Cow Now Be - fore she goes to bed." The

Dai - ry-maid She curtsied, And went and told The Al - der-ney:
poco cresc.
"Don't for-get the but - ter for The Roy - al slice of bread." The
p
poco rit.
Al - der-ney Said sleep-i - ly, "You'd bet-ter tell His Ma-jes-ty That
p poco rit.
p
accel.
man - y peo - ple now - a - days Like mar - ma - lade in - stead."
accel.
mf

The
a tempo
dim.
Dai - ry-maid Said, "Fan-cy!" And went_ to Her Ma - jes - ty; She
curt - sied to the Queen and She turned a lit - tle red: "Ex -
- cuse me, Your Ma - jes - ty, For tak - ing of The li - ber - ty, But

mar - ma-lade is tas - ty if It's ve - ry Thick-ly Spread." The
p
Queen said "Oh!" And went to His Ma - jes-ty: "Talk-ing of the but-ter for The
poco cresc.
p
Roy-al slice of bread, Man - y peo-ple Think that Mar-ma-lade Is ni - cer.
poco rit.
poco rit.
p
a tempo
Would you like to try a lit - tle Mar - ma-lade In-stead?"
a tempo
cresc.
mf

The King said, "Bo-ther!" And
cresc.
mf
then he said, "Oh, dear - y me!" The King sobbed,"Oh, dear - y me!" And
p
went back to bed. "No - bo-dy," he whim-pered, "Could
mf
call me A fuss-y man; I on-ly want A lit-tle bit Of
f
p

but-ter for My bread!" The Queen said, "There, there!" And
p
poco cresc.
went to The Dair-y-maid; The Dair-y-maid Said, "There, there!" And
3
3
p
went to the shed. The cow said, "There, there! I did-n't real-ly Mean it; Here's
p
milk for his por-rin-ger And but-ter for his bread."
mf

The
Queen took The but-ter And brought it to His Ma-jes-ty;
The King said, "Butter, eh!" And bounced out of bed.
dim.
mp
f
p
poco cresc.
"No-bo-dy," he said, As he kissed her Ten-der-ly—

* These two bars are for use only when the dance is not required.

The Court Musician strikes up a merry tune.–

Allegro.

mf

The King says

"Stop! this is not stately enough!"

Tempo di Menuetto.

p

p
cresc.
p
cresc.
p
sf

I do — like a lit - tle bit of but-ter to my bread.
p
f
cresc.
ff

FEED-MY-COW

FEED - MY - COW
Very simply
Verses 1-8
I went down to feed-my-cow, (Feed-my-cow, Feed-my-cow) I went down to feed my cow At ten o'-clock in the morn-ning.
She looked out and shook-her-head, (Shook-her-head, Shook-her-head) She looked out and shook her head At ten o'-clock in the morn-ning.
mf
p
cresc.

I went down to feed–my–cow,
(Feed–my–cow,
Feed–my–cow)
I went down to feed my cow
At ten o'clock in the morning.

She looked out and shook–her–head,
(Shook–her–head,
Shook–her–head)
She looked out and shook her head,
At ten o'clock in the morning.

I said boldly "Here–I–come!"
(Here–I–come,
Here–I–come)
I said boldly "Here I come,
At ten o'clock in the morning."

She looked out and shook–her–horns,
(Shook–her–horns,
Shook–her–horns)
She looked out and shook her horns
At ten o'clock in the morning.

I said bravely "Not–so–close!"
(Not–so–close,
Not–so–close)
I said bravely "Not so close,
At ten o'clock in the morning."

She came out and shook–her–tail,
(Shook–her–tail,
Shook–her–tail)
She came out and shook her tail
At ten o'clock in the morning.

I went back to ask–the–time,
(Ask–the–time,
Ask–the–time)
I went back to ask the time
At ten o'clock in the morning.

She came too, to ask–the–time,
(Ask–the–time,
Ask–the–time)
She came too, to ask the time
At ten o'clock in the morning.

We both ran, but I–asked–first,
(I–asked–first,
I–asked–first)
We both ran, but I asked first.
'Twas ten o'clock in the morning.

FOURTEEN SONGS
from
WHEN WE WERE VERY YOUNG

Dedicated by permission

of

H.R.H. PRINCESS MARY
VISCOUNTESS LASCELLES

to the

AUTOCRATS OF HER NURSERY

CONTENTS

&

Happiness

Happily
John had great big wa-ter-proof Boots on;
John had a great big wa-ter proof Hat; John had a great big wa-ter proof Mac-in-tosh
And that (said John) Is That.

Missing

Wistfully
Has an - y - bod - y seen my mouse?
p
I o - pened his box for half a min - ute, Just to make sure he was
real - ly in it, And while I was look - ing, he jumped out - side! I tried to catch him, I
tried, I tried, I think he's some - where a - bout the house. Has an - y - one seen my
mf

Suspiciously
Wistfully again
mouse? Un-cle John, have you seen_ my mouse?
Just a small sort of mouse, a
dear lit-tle brown one, He came from the coun-try, he was-n't a town one; So he'll feel all lone-ly in a
Lon-don street; Why, what could he pos-si-bly find to eat? He must be somewhere. I'll ask Aunt Rose: Have
A last hope
mf
you seen a mouse with a wof-fel-ly nose?
Oh! some-where a-bout He's
just got out.
Despairingly
Has-n't an-y-bod-y seen my mouse?_
rit.

In the Fashion

"Let me try one," I'd say to the el-e-phant, "This is my one." They'd all come round to
cresc.
see.
f
Proudly
mf
Then I'd
say to the li-on, "Why, you've got a tail! And so has the el-e-phant, and so has the whale! And,
look! There's a croc-o-dile! He's got a tail! "You've all got tails like me!"
cresc.
Triumphantly
f
f

Halfway Down

Half-way up the stairs Is-n't up, And is-n't down. It
is-n't in the nur-ser-y, It is-n't in the town; And
all sorts of fun-ny thoughts Run round my head: "It
is-n't real-ly an-y-where! It's some-where else In-stead!"
It is-n't real-ly an-y-where! It's some-where else in-stead!
poco rit.
p a tempo
mp
ten.
ten.
mp
Slightly slower
p

Hoppity

Animato again (which in this case means "Jigging up and down")
f
dim.
Chris - to - pher Rob - in goes Hop - pi - ty, hop - pi - ty, Hop - pi - ty,
mf
hop - pi - ty, hop.
When - ev - er I tell him Po -
f
mf
-lite - ly to stop it, he says he can't pos - si - bly stop.

Slacken speed
If he stopped hop - ping, he could - n't go an - y - where, Poor lit - tle Chris - to - pher
mf
In time
could - n't go an - y - where_ That's why he al - ways goes Hop - pi - ty, hop - pi - ty,
Now then, much faster
Hop - pi - ty, Hop - pi - ty, Hop. Hop - pi - ty
Quickening
f much faster
Hop - pi - ty, Hop - pi - ty, Hop - pi - ty, Hop - pi - ty,
Hop - pi - ty, Hop.
sf

Growing Up

Brightly (as befits a man with braces)
mf
con Ped.
I've got shoes_ with grown-up laces, I've got knick-ers and a pair of bra-ces, I'm all read-y to
poco rit.
a tempo
run some rac-es. Who's com-ing out with me?
I've got a nice_ new pair of bra-ces, I've got shoes with

new brown la - ces, I know won - der - ful pad - dly plac - es,
poco rit.
Who's com - ing out with me?
a tempo
Slightly slower
Ev - 'ry morn - ing my new grace is, "Thank you, God for my new bra - ces;
mp
I can tie my new brown la - ces." Who's com - ing out with
cresc.
poco rit.
Up to time
mf a tempo
me?

Buckingham Palace
In march time
They're changing guard at Buck-ing-ham Pal-ace
Chris-to-pher Ro-bin went down with Al-ice.
Al-ice is mar-ry-ing one of the guard. "A sol-dier's life is ter-ri-ble hard,"
Says Al-ice.
They're chang-ing guard at Buck-ing-ham Palace
f
stacc.
mf
sf

Chris-to-pher Ro-bin went down with Al-ice. We
saw a guard in a sen-try-box. "One of the sergeants looks af-ter their socks," Says
Al-ice. They're chang-ing guard at Buck-ing-ham Pal-ace—
Chris-to-pher Rob-in went down with Al-ice. We
looked for the King, but he nev-er came. "Well, God take care of him, all the same," Says

Al-ice.
They're chang-ing guard at Buck-ing-ham Pal-ace_
Chris-to-pher Rob-in went down with Al-ice.
They've
great big par-ties in-side the grounds."I would-n't be King for a hun-dred pounds,"
Says
Al-ice.
They're chang-ing guard at Buck-ing-ham Pal-ace
Chris-to-pher Rob-in went down with Al-ice
A
sf
mf

face looked out, but it was-n't the King's. "He's much too bus-y a sign-ing things," Says
Al-ice. They're chang-ing guard at Buck-ing-ham Pal-ace_
Chris-to-pher Rob-in went down with Al-ice "Do
you think the King knows all a-bout *me?*" "Sure to, dear, but it's time_ for tea,"
Says Al-ice.

The Three Foxes

2. They lived in the for - est in three lit - tle hous - es, And they
4. They went to a fair, and they all won priz - es
p
didn't wear coats, and they didn't wear trous - es They
Three plum pud-ding-ses and three mince pie - ses. They
ran through the woods on their lit - tle bare toot-sies. And they played "Touch last" with a
rode on el - e - phants and swang on swing-ses, And hit three co-coa-nuts at
poco cresc.
fam - i - ly of mous - es.
co - coa - nut shie - ses.
mf
1.
3. They

12.
5. That's all that I know of the three little foxes Who
kept their handkerchiefs in cardboard boxes
They
lived in the forest in three littel houses, But they didn't wear coats and they
didn't wear trouses, And they didn't wear stockings and they didn't wear sockses.
p
cresc.
f
Ped.
Ped.

Politeness

Politely, and so don't hurry it
If people ask me, I always tell them: "Quite well, thank you, I'm very glad to say." If people ask me, I always answer, "Quite well, thank you, how are you to-day?"
fp rather staccato
mp
p
fp
I always answer, I always tell them, If they ask me Po-lite-ly
In confidence
BUT SOMETIMES I wish That they would-n't.
pp
pp

Market Square
Not too fast, or Aunt Susan won't hear all the words.
1. I had a pen-ny, A bright new pen-ny I
3. I found a six-pence, A lit-tle white six-pence I
mf
took my pen-ny To the mar-ket square. I wan-ted a rab-bit, A lit-tle brown rab-bit, And I
took it in my hand To the mar-ket square. I was buy-ing my rab-bit, I do like rab-bits, And I
looked for a rab-bit 'Most ev-'ry-where. For I went to the stall where they sold sweet lav-en-der
looked for my rab-bit 'Most ev-'ry-where. So I went to the stall where they sold fine sauce-pans
Sadly
"On-ly a pen-ny for a bunch of lav-en-der!" Have you got a rab-bit, 'cos I don't want lavender? But they
"Walk up, walk up, sixpence for a sauce-pan!" "Could I have a rab-bit, 'cos we've got two saucepans? But they
p

had-n't got a rab-bit, not an-y-where there.
had-n't got a rab-bit, not an-y-where there.
2. I had a pen-ny, And I
4. I had nuff-in, No, I
p
had an-o-ther pen-ny I took my pennies To the mar-ket square. I did want a rab-bit, A
had-n't got nuff-in', So I did-n't go down To the mar-ket square. But I walked on the com-mon, The
4th Verse
Faster.
lit-tle ba-by rab-bit And I looked for rab-bits 'Most ev-'ry-where. And I went to the stall where they
old-gold common And I saw lit-tle rab-bits 'Most ev-'ry-where! So I'm sor-ry for the peo-ple who
sold fresh mackerel (Now then! Tuppence for a fresh caught mackerel!) "Have you got a rab-bit 'cos I
sell fine saucepans, I'm sor-ry for the peo-ple who sell fresh mackerel, I'm sor-ry for the peo-ple who
4th Verse
In a whisper.
2nd Verse only.
last Verse.
don't like mackerel? But they hadn't got a rabbit not anywhere there.
sell sweet lavender, 'Cos they haven't got a rabbit not anywhere there.
p
pp

The Christening

Very deliberately
end of his back. And I some-times call him Ter-ri-ble James, 'Cos he
says he likes me call-ing him names.
cresc. e rit.
f
in time
p
Lovingly
But I think, I think I shall
dim.
p a little slower
call him Jim, 'Cos I am so fond of him.
mf
in time
dim.
p
pp

Brownie

Timidly, with one eye on nurse
mf
dim.
mp
In a corn - er of the bed - room is a great big cur - tain,
Some - one lives be - hind it. but I don't know who; I
think it is a Brown - ie but I'm not quite cer - tain.

Awed
(Nan - ny is - n't cer - tain too.)
mf
dim.
I looked be - hind the cur - tain, but he
mp
went so quick - ly Brown - ies nev - er wait to say, "How d'you do?" They
cresc.
wrig - gle off at once be - cause they're all so tick - ly.
mf
Importantly
(Nan - ny says they're tick - ly
mp
too.)
p

Lines and Squares.

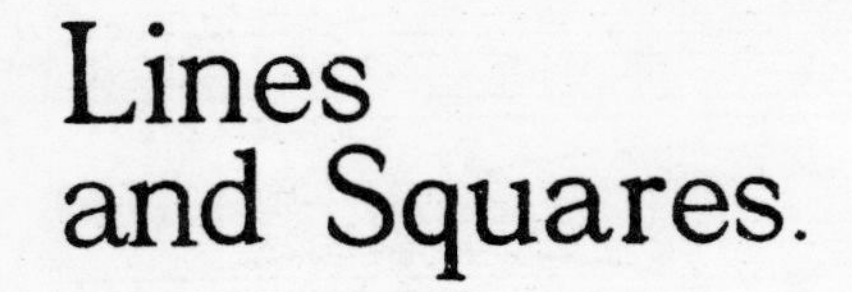

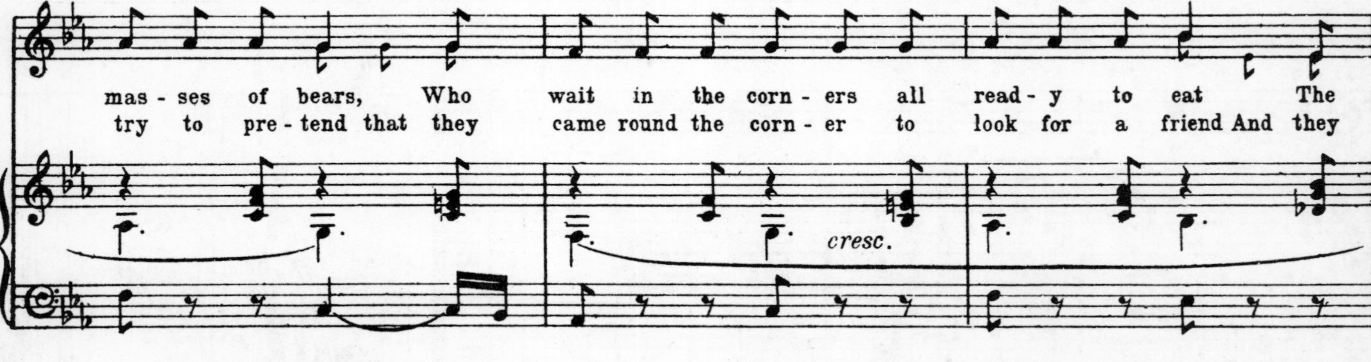

1.
sil - lies who tread on the lines of the street, Go back to their lairs,
try to pre - tend that
And I say to them "Bears, Just
look how I'm walk - ing in all of the squares."
f
2.
no - bod - y cares wheth - er you walk in the lines or squares, But

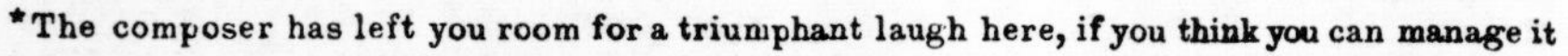
*The composer has left you room for a triumphant laugh here, if you think you can manage it

Vespers
Sleepily
Lit - tle Boy kneels at the foot of the bed,
Droops on the lit - tle hands lit - tle gold head.
Hush! Hush! Whis - per who dares!
Chris - to - pher Rob - in is say - ing his prayers.
God bless Mum - my. I

A little faster
know that's right. Was - n't it fun in the bath to - night? The
cresc.
Slower again
cold's so cold, and the hot's so hot. Oh! God bless Dad - dy I
mf
p
Quickening
quite for - got. If I o - pen my fing - ers a lit - tle bit more, I can
cresc.
see Nan - ny's dress - ing - gown on the door. It's a beau - ti - ful blue, but it
mf
Slower
has - n't a hood. Oh! God bless Nan - ny and make her good.
p

again quickening
Mine has a hood, and I lie in bed, And
mp
pull the hood right o - ver my head, And I shut my eyes, and I
curl up small, And no - bod - y knows that I'm there at all. Oh!
p
A little slower
Quickening
Thank you, God, for a love - ly day. And what was the o - ther I
cresc.
had to say? I said "Bless Dad - dy," so what can it be? Oh!
mf

Slower
rit.
Sleepily again
Now I re - mem - ber it God bless Me.
Lit - tle Boy kneels at the
p
rit.
p a tempo
foot of the bed,
Droops on the lit - tle hands lit - tle gold head.
More and more sleepily
Hush! Hush! Whis - per who dares!
Chris - to - pher Rob - in is
pp
Out on tip-toe; he's asleep
say - ing his prayers.
pp
ppp